Pet of the Met

Also by Lydia and Don Freeman

CHUGGY AND THE BLUE CABOOSE

PET of the MET

BY LYDIA AND DON FREEMAN

PUFFIN BOOKS

PUFFIN BOOKS
Published by the Penguin Group
Viking Penguin Inc., 40 West 23rd Street, New York, New York 10010, U.S.A.
Penguin Books Ltd, 27 Wrights Lane, London W8 5TZ England
Penguin Books Australia Ltd, Ringwood, Victoria, Australia
Penguin Books Canada Ltd, 2801 John Street, Markham, Ontario, Canada L3R 1B4
Penguin Books (N.Z.) Ltd, 182–190 Wairau Road, Auckland 10, New Zealand

Penguin Books Ltd, Registered Offices: Harmondsworth, Middlesex, England

First published in the United States of America by Viking Penguin Inc., 1953
Published in Seafarer 1972
Published in Picture Puffins 1988

Color separations by Imago Ltd., Hong Kong
Printed in the United States of America by Lake Book/Cuneo, Melrose Park, Illinois

Copyright Lydia and Don Freeman, 1953
Copyright © renewed Lydia Freeman, 1981
All rights reserved
Library of Congress catalog card number: 87-63521
ISBN 0-14-050892-9

Pet of the Met

High up in the attic of the Metropolitan Opera House, in a forgotten harp case, there once lived a white mouse named Maestro Petrini.

With him lived Madame Petrini and their three teeny-weeny Petrinis, Doe, Ray, and Mee.

Next to his family Maestro Petrini loved the opera more than anything else in the world. He knew all the opera stories by heart and could hum most of the music.

This was not surprising because he worked for his daily cheese downstairs in the Opera House itself.

Here he is, working as a page turner for the Prompter, in the Prompter's box.

The Prompter's box is a small cavelike place set in the center of the stage footlights. No one in the audience ever sees or hears the Prompter, but he is a very important man. The singers watch and listen to him, for they depend upon him to help them remember the words of their songs if they should ever forget.

The Prompter was always careful to keep Maestro Petrini well hidden behind the big music book, and for two good reasons: first, singers are not exactly partial to mice; and second, the Prompter knew of a

certain cat, named Mefisto, who lived in the basement just below. Mefisto lived in an empty violin
case, but he hated music more than anything else in
the world, except mice.

Every time he heard singing from upstairs he would try to shut out the sound. He wouldn't even let himself listen to find out whether or not he liked it. He was just plain prejudiced against music.

Every night after the performance it was his job to rid the great Opera House of mice. This is how he earned his daily bowl of milk. It was an easy job because he never found any victims.

The Opera House was so enormous that Mefisto had never discovered the attic high at the top. This was fortunate for the carefree Petrinis.

During his spare time Maestro Petrini would put on his own opera performances with his family as the cast. Of all the operas their favorite was *The Magic Flute* by Mozart.

The Magic Flute is about a prince who, with a magic flute to protect him, searches for his princess throughout the realm of the Queen of the Night. A funny birdcatcher named Papageno helps him to find his way. Whenever they are in danger the music of the magic flute charms even the most ferocious animals of the forest. This is how they are able to make their way safely through every trial.

CHEESE BOX

Maestro Petrini took great delight in playing the
part of the foolish birdcatcher. Madame Petrini had
made his costume out of an old feather duster she had
found in the corner of the attic.

Madame Petrini herself preferred to play the Queen
of the Night. She made her costume out of some dark-
blue cheesecloth she just happened to have handy.

The scene they all liked best was the one in which the ferocious animals of the forest dance to the music of the magic flute. You can imagine who whistled like a flute!

For this scene Doe dressed up as a lion by wearing a mop and tying a tassel to the end of his tail. Ray became a rabbit by folding back his ears and tying his tail into a bunny-knot. As for Mee, he merely put on his mother's green spectacles and painted stripes around his tail. You couldn't tell him from a tiger!

They danced this scene so hard and so long that they never were able to finish the rest of the opera, no matter how early they had started.

One day just after an especially wonderful dancing scene, the teeny-weeny Petrinis gathered around their papa and breathlessly pleaded, "Please, Papa, when can we go downstairs and see you act in the real opera?"

24

SPECIAL
CHILDREN'S
OPERA MATINEE
performance
of
MOZARTS'
MAGIC
FLUTE

That very evening as they sat down to an elegant cheese-soufflé supper, Papa Petrini gave his family a surprise and a promise. They would all be permitted to attend a Special Children's Opera matinee the next day. It was to be *The Magic Flute!*

First thing the next morning Madame Petrini set about washing everybody's ears. She wanted to make sure that not a single note would be missed!

Maestro Petrini combed his hair and curled his whiskers, a process which took most of the morning.

Meanwhile, downstairs, Mefisto, the cat, suspected that something extraordinary was going on that afternoon. He went prowling around backstage, searching for you know who! When he peeked through the peephole in the curtain

this is what he saw. The children were already beginning to arrive for the matinee!

Upstairs in the attic at this very moment the Petrinis were setting out, all primped and powdered and on their best behavior.

Maestro Petrini had to let his family find their own seats while he hurried off to his Prompter's box to get ready for the performance.

Soon every seat in the entire Opera House was filled.
But where are Madame Petrini and Doe, Ray, Mee?

Here they are! They have found themselves a perfect place. What could be better than to snuggle behind a young lady's white gloves?

Gradually the lights all over the house dimmed down. Everyone was silent and expectant.

The orchestra conductor appeared and made one long deep bow.

Then the overture began

Just before the great golden curtains parted, the Prompter leaned over and whispered into his partner's ear, "We must be especially good today, my pet. Boys and girls deserve the very best, you know!"

Then the curtain went up. The opera was under way!

When Papageno, the foolish birdcatcher, appeared
and began to sing

the audience was all eyes and ears.

And when the Prince played upon his flute, one by one the stage animals came out and danced to the magic music.

But look! Can it be? Yes, it is!
Maestro Petrini, completely carried away
by the music, has leaped out of his box
before the Prompter can
stop him!

He's dancing! And what's more he is dancing in perfect rhythm to the music!

Of course none of the children in the audience can see the tiny Maestro dancing. But his family can. They are taking turns looking through a pair of opera glasses left resting on the velvet railing. And to tell the awful truth, someone else is watching! The cat, Mefisto! He watches from the dark side-curtains backstage!

"Petrini! Run for your life!" shouts the Prompter.

Out springs Mefisto.

In and out about the stage Mefisto chases Petrini. Through the dancers' legs they speed like streaks of lightning, while the flute music grows more and more beautiful and exciting until

poor Petrini is caught by his coat tail! But wait—

The strangest thing is happening.

What can it be?

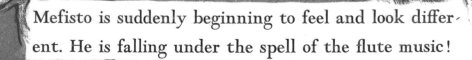

Mefisto is suddenly beginning to feel and look different. He is falling under the spell of the flute music!

Now *he*'s dancing! And dancing! Never in the history of the Metropolitan has there been such a scene — such waltzing and turning — such feline grace!

Even after the music had stopped Mefisto and Petrini continued to whirl and twirl until the curtain had to be brought down.

When the audience called for more, Maestro Petrini felt obliged to step out in front of the curtain and make several deep, dignified bows.

The Prompter reached out and pulled him back into the box. This broke the spell for Petrini.

The Prompter was very angry. "See here, my pet," he scolded, "you made me lose my place in the music book. You'll have to decide now, once and for all, whether you intend to be an opera star or a page-turner. You simply can't be both! I have a good notion to hire Mefisto the cat."

"Oh no, no!" pleaded Petrini. "I'll be your page-turner and I promise never to be an opera star again!"

That afternoon when the performance was over, a subdued and humbled Maestro returned to his home in the harp case. There, to his great surprise, his family showered him with bravos and squeals of applause! They told him his performance had been the best part of the opera!

"And the cat was pretty funny, too!" said Doe. "The flute certainly tamed him down — and just in the nick of time!" To this remark Papa Petrini said nothing. He was hungry. And he had brought home a special present from his friend the Prompter — an extra-large portion of Swiss cheese!

Far down in the basement another opera lover was exhausted but happy. Mefisto, forgetting for the first time about ridding the house of mice, had his supper and went straight to bed in his violin case. He purred himself to sleep with a tune from *The Magic Flute*.

As you might guess, Maestro Petrini and Mister Mefisto soon became good friends. And to this day it is said that between them they have the run of the entire Metropolitan Opera House!